The
Wind Garden

For Antje with love – AM
For Benjamin and his parents – CF

A Red Fox Book

Published by Random House Children's Books
20 Vauxhall Bridge Road, London SW1V 2SA

A division of Random House UK Ltd
London Melbourne Sydney Auckland
Johannesburg and agencies throughout the world

Copyright © text Angela McAllister 1994
Copyright © illustrations Claire Fletcher 1994

1 3 5 7 9 10 8 6 4 2

First published in Great Britain by
The Bodley Head Children's Books 1994

Red Fox edition 1996

Printed in Singapore

RANDOM HOUSE UK Limited Reg. No. 954009

ISBN 0 09 968351 2

The Wind Garden

Angela McAllister &
Claire Fletcher

Red Fox

Grandpa lived at the top of a high house. His old legs wouldn't take him up and down the long staircase any more, so he stayed at home. Ellie came to visit every day.

'I miss the park, Ellie,' said Grandpa. 'I miss walking in the gardens.'

So Ellie brought some seeds and flowerpots. Together they planted the seeds, put them out on Grandpa's roof and waited.

The seeds sprouted. They grew thin little stems and tiny leaves. But out on the roof the wind was always blowing. The seedlings couldn't grow in the wind and they died.

'That bad old wind,' said Ellie. 'Where does it come from Grandpa?'

'No one can guess,' said Grandpa, 'nobody knows, where the wind comes from, where the wind goes.'

Ellie brought sunflowers to make a garden for Grandpa. Together they put them out on the roof and watered each one. The flowers grew up and up towards the sun.

But out on the roof the wind was always blowing. It rocked the sunflowers, harder and harder, until their tall stems broke.

'That wicked old wind,' said Ellie. 'Where is it blowing to Grandpa?'

'No one can guess, nobody knows, where the wind comes from, where the wind goes,' said Grandpa. 'I think that old wind is just trying to tell me I live too high in the sky for a garden.'

That night Ellie stayed at Grandpa's house. In bed she could hear the wind blowing. Ellie went out on the roof in Grandpa's big nightshirt.

The wind danced around her. Round and round it rushed, until Ellie was dancing too. And with a great gust the wind lifted Ellie up, off Grandpa's roof, and into the starry sky.

'I'm going to where the wind blows!' laughed Ellie, and she wished Grandpa was flying too.

Soon she came to a little wood on a mountain top. The wind gently set her down. Ellie saw that all the trees were hung with things the wind had carried away; kites and balloons, hats and handkerchiefs, coloured flags, church bells and lost washing.

It was the wind's garden.

The wind blew proudly, it made everything flutter and dance. It made everything rustle and chime, swinging, spinning, shimmering in the sun. Ellie whirled among the trees.

'If only Grandpa could see the wind garden,' she laughed.

Ellie saw a kite she had lost long ago. As she took its tail the wind lifted her up and carried her back to Grandpa's house.

The next day Grandpa sat, remembering, out on his empty roof.

Ellie brought a box. Together they pulled out flags and chimes, stars and sparkling suns, windmills and bells and spinning things.

'Here is your garden, Grandpa,' she said. 'Here is a garden to share with the wind.'

Out on the roof the wind was always blowing. It made everything swing, spin and shimmer in the sun.

Grandpa smiled, 'No one can guess, nobody knows, where the wind comes from, where the wind goes...'

Somebody knew. Ellie knew.

But Ellie wasn't going to tell.

Some bestselling Red Fox picture books

THE BIG ALFIE AND ANNIE ROSE STORYBOOK
by Shirley Hughes
OLD BEAR
by Jane Hissey
OI! GET OFF OUR TRAIN
by John Burningham
DON'T DO THAT!
by Tony Ross
NOT NOW, BERNARD
by David McKee
ALL JOIN IN
by Quentin Blake
THE WHALES' SONG
by Gary Blythe and Dyan Sheldon
JESUS' CHRISTMAS PARTY
by Nicholas Allan
THE PATCHWORK CAT
by Nicola Bayley and William Mayne
MATILDA
by Hilaire Belloc and Posy Simmonds
WILLY AND HUGH
by Anthony Browne
THE WINTER HEDGEHOG
by Ann and Reg Cartwright
A DARK, DARK TALE
by Ruth Brown
HARRY, THE DIRTY DOG
by Gene Zion and Margaret Bloy Graham
DR XARGLE'S BOOK OF EARTHLETS
by Jeanne Willis and Tony Ross
WHERE'S THE BABY?
by Pat Hutchins